What Would You Do If Your Pastor Was A

Homosexual?

Apostle Carolyn Edwards

Printed in the United States of America.

ISBN: 0615726615
ISBN-13: 978-0615726618

Published & Distributed By:
Doors of Life

Cover Design & Formatting:
NyShell Imari Unlimited
www.nyshellimari.com

Dedication

This book is dedicated to you - Redemption Fellowship, True Anointing Deliverance Ministry, Faithful Few Spiritual Church 1&2, Zion Daughter and Faith and Deliverance Ministry. Only God knew this day would come for us to be able to worship freely, walking in the spirit of truth. Through all the church services we share together the good times, the pain as well as the deliverance that always took the service to a whole new level in Christ. We all suffered when God removed family members from our midst and took them home to Glory. I know we have had lots of trials and tribulations through the years, but yet we are still standing strong against the enemy. I want to thank all of my sons and daughters (Pastoral Leaders) who chose to come out of the closet and face the truth about the sin of homosexuality - to God be the Glory. God longs for us to stay faithful to His word and discover the sanctified life that He divinely orchestrated and created for us to live here on earth.

"Before I formed thee in the belly I knew thee; and before thou camest forth out of the womb I sanctified thee, and I ordained thee a prophet unto the nations." - Jeremiah 1:5

Acknowledgements

I'm grateful to the hundreds of writers and teachers, both spiritual and natural, who assisted in shaping my life. I thank God for my husband Bishop Lyle Edwards, my daughter Duchess LyAsiah Edwards, niece Tamika Thurman and sisters in Christ Kim Milton and NyShell Imari. A special thanks to Miller and Carmen Thomas along with my entire family, both spiritual and natural, for the privilege of trusting me with your life stories.

Love Always,

Apostle Edwards

Table of Contents

Introduction

Chapter 1   5

Chapter 2   11

Chapter 3   17

Chapter 4   29

Chapter 5   35

Chapter 6   41

Chapter 7   45

Chapter 8   47

Introduction

This book is the first of a series of books that will focus on exposing homosexuality. We will address some of the world's views on spiritual and personal beliefs concerning homosexuality. My experimental research on gay men and lesbian women has awakened and enlightened me in a way that will be life changing to all who read about it. This book will assist those in the body of Christ in understanding the spirit of homosexuality. Many people have stated that the homosexual spirit came straight from the pit of hell, others say that they were born that way but the most alarming fact in this matter is that many just wanted to try having sex with the same sex, but it turned out that it wasn't for them. You will find that this book is biblically backed by the Holy Scriptures.

In my twenty-five years of research in this area, I found out that many people who lived the homosexual lifestyle all had one thing in common; they all agreed that they have been delivered from the unclean homosexual spirit. The spectacular part of the research is that many of those people are leaders in ministry. While reading this book you must have an open mind as God leads us on this journey.

" For this cause God gave them up unto vile affections: for even their women did change the natural use into that which is against nature: And likewise also the men, leaving the natural use of the woman, burned in their lust one toward another; men with men working that which is unseemly, and receiving in themselves that recompense of their error which was meet."
Romans 1:26-27

"For the wages of sin is death; but the gift of God is eternal life through Jesus Christ our Lord."
Romans 6:23

Chapter 1

Exposing the Spirit of Homosexuality

The unclean, shameful, homosexual spirit has destroyed the church, jobs, homes and millions of families. When families have to split because of this spirit, it divides with no intention of hope or reconciliation. Our society is over saturated with homosexuality; unfortunately much of what is depicted in the media regarding sexuality comes with no cost. People in this day and age have no clue that the enemy is in full control of their lives. Sexuality is three-dimensional; it deals with spirit, body and soul. When sexual purpose intended by God is reestablished, we can focus on the true spiritual nature of sexual intimacy.

Most Christians turn their nose up at the mention of the word "homo" - these are people that want to be deep in the body of Christ. Most believers don't want to involve themselves with same sex marriages or partnerships. The family as God ordained it; walls tumble down after discovering homosexuality was lurking in their homes. One thing to know is we as a people need to recognize that sin and rebellion will always destroy us. God will expose anything that is hiding in the dark and bring it to the light. Many Pastors of the cloth are out of order when they refuse

5

to deal head on with this spirit that has infested our world. God's man or woman of the cloth must continue to declare that we were all created in an image of holiness. I am not just talking about believers, there are many sinners who want to come to church to get their lives together, but after church most of the "Christians" join them in the street, (dropping it like it's hot). The people of God are not realizing they are actually losing souls and that they are going to be held accountable for, which means the blood is on you. People that always need someone else's approval will never mature to a place of leadership.

I would like to share a story with you of a young bisexual man in a church service in Birmingham, Alabama. He came through the church doors pimping as if he was looking for a woman, but there was a bisexual choir singing at that service. When the singing started the church went up in the spirit of praise. In addition, he sought after the Holy Spirit where with he made a connection, but he noticed the bisexual men worshiping God differently. For example their foot-work in praise and body movements. He also saw the way the homosexuals poked their lips out, in a sexual manner. As the shouting was going on in the sanctuary, he stopped praising God and started shouting like the gay men in that service. The young man wanted to be noticed by the bisexual men in that church service. The enemy's job is to make a person think they are in control of their spiritual atmosphere, when the butt-naked truth is, he was caught up in a black spider web from the pit of hell. He left the church service with a gay man; let us just say he is a big part of the gay inner circle now.

When I see church people performing for flesh not God, they are full of you know what! Please let your mind tap into what I am trying to say for one minute, I promise you baby, you were never ready for this! God has renewed my mindset, I am saved for real, if I wasn't saved, I would have spelled the word out for you to read. But when you get delivered from sin, God leaves no stones unturned. Let us move on with this knowledge God is downloading in us.

You know many church people in this world can never be wrong about the word of God because His spirit only dwells in them and that is why you have no friends today. Come on say what you feel, I got God and that is all I need, you lie. Please do not judge me, I Love Shiloh, Alpha and Omega, Lord of Lords, Rose of Sharon, the True Witness of my soul. You must know who people are in the kingdom of God - We have baby Christians, deep church folk, prophets, saints and everybody else that want to be great in the body of Christ. The one thing that always trips me out about some so-called saints is they will get mad at you, if you   forget to call them Bishop, Apostle, Pastor, Prophet or whatever their title might be. My question is did God ordain them or did men make them? *It's tight, but it's right.* Check this out, if you were truly ordained by God "A man's gift maketh room for him, and bringeth him before great men" (Proverbs 18:16). Because I forgot your title, that so call sanctified spirit in you might want to send me to hell but it's not about you!

Church used to be known as the hospital for sick people. James 5:14 says "Is any sick among you? Let him call for the elders of the church; and let them pray over him, anointing him with old in the name of the Lord." Well as time has passed, now church as we know it is long gone, it has become like Corporate America. God fearing people say that they love the Lord with all their hearts, but the problem is they do not like God's people. Most Pastors currently do not operate in deliverance according to Matthew 15:24-26 which says "But He answer and said, I am not sent but unto the lost sheep of the house of Israel. Then came she and worshipped him, saying Lord help me! But He answered and said, it is not meat to take the children's bread, and cast it to the dogs" and a demonic spirit better not speak out loud in the midst of service where deliverance should take place. You will find yourself alone battling demonic forces by yourself. Many people serve in their church in the choir, praise team, usher board, etc. The only problem I have is their attitude towards other people is so bad.

Have you ever run into a rude so-called saint in the sanctuary and you needed their help? "A man that has friends must show himself friendly: and there is a friend that sticketh closer than a brother" (Proverbs 18:24). Have you ever met someone that always has a word from the Lord and God has already told them what you are about to say and you can't get a word. into the conversation? I'm scared of them! On the other hand, a lot of Christians are still on infant formula (milk) when it comes to homosexuality. Church people were under the assumption that the curse of homosexuality would pass through to one of their own family members if they would have fellowship with any gay person. The people had no knowledge about gay men and lesbian women, so they acted out of character every time a homosexual individual came around. Let me be frank with you, a sinner doesn't need you to tell them about their sin that is why they came to church for help. Nevertheless, we the people of God gave them more pain so they went back to the streets where they were accepted and received true love. Remember, God is the God of second chances, grace and mercy always shows it's face, when sin is in the camp.

Apostle Carolyn Edwards

Chapter 2

Was I Born That Way or Made That Way?

P eople always wonder if a person can be born gay - According to the bible in Judges 19, it talks about a Levite man who had a concubine that played the harlot and went away to her father's house. After four months, her husband the Levite man arose and went after her, to speak kindly to her and bring her back home. Then it came to pass on the fourth day the Levite man was ready to depart; but the young woman's father said to his son-in-law, refresh your heart with a morsel of bread and afterward go your way, but the Levite man ate and drank. Then the woman's father said to the man, please allow yourself to be content to stay all night, and let your heart be merry. Then on the fifth day, the Levite man was ready to depart from his father-in-law's house but they delayed until the afternoon and both the Levite man and his concubine ate dinner with the man of the house. Time came for the Levite, his concubine and his servant's departure but his wife's father tried to delay their departure again by informing him the day is now drawing toward evening. However, the man was not willing to spend that night, so he rose and departed.

To make a long story short, the Levite man, his concubine, servant and two saddled donkeys were near a place called Jebus (that is, Jerusalem) the city of the Jebusites and the servant asked his master if they could lodge there for the night. The servant's master said to him, we will not turn into a city of a foreigners who are not of the children of Israel, the sun went down on them near Gibeah and Ramah so they turned aside there to go in to lodge in Gibeah for the night. The Levite man and his family went in and sat down in the open square of the city, for no one would take them into his house to spend the night. The custom of that time was when a person needed to spend the night in a city you had to go in the middle of that city and wait until someone invited you in their home for the night and whoever was with you they had to have enough food to feed your animals and the people that were with you.

Just then an old man came in from his work in the field at evening, who was also from the mountain of Ephraim; he was staying in Gibeah the home of the Benjamites. The old man saw the traveler and enquired to the Levite "Where did you come from and where are you on your way to?" He stated, "We are passing from Bethlehem in Judah toward the remote mountain." Ephraim, the old man, said "I am from there. I went to Bethlehem in Judah; now I am going to the house of the Lord. But there is no one who will take me into his house, although we have both straw and fodder for our donkeys, and bread and wine for myself, for your female servant, and for the young man who is with your servant; there is no lack of anything." The old man said, "Peace be with you! However let all your needs be my responsibility; only do not spend the night in the open square." Favor is not fair, but I got it.

The enemy has set so many of God's people up in this world. People felt like life was easier when they were in the street turning tricks to make ends meet; the butt-naked truth is your life and family has always given you a hard time. My mother told me if you ever meet a person that has been through hell all there life, they have a powerful calling on them from on High. One of the problems in this world is that when a person's spiritual gifts kick in, there is no one around to activate their God given gift. Activation is when you need someone that operates in the pure indoctrinated deliverance. Most pastor's best friends and some of their family members cannot explain to them what they are going through, only because they will not let go of past hurts, pain and relationships. Because of this, God cannot fill them up will his Holy Ghost power. In addition, some people are trapped in bondage from their past life and feel like God cannot use them because they have damaged and destroyed many things, including people's lives. They do not want to go far in Christ because they only see, think, and feel failure. Boo shake yourself loose!

If you ever have to talk to somebody that has been to jail or got caught stealing, the first thing they will say is "Something told me not to go, do it or steal that day. If I had just listened to my mother and not my friends and followed my own mind, I would not be in this mess today." We need to know on a daily basis we are warring against two spirits within our body, good and bad. The sad part about warring in the spirit is that most Christians do not know the difference between God's voice and the devil's voice. God is not going to tell you to do wrong and the devil will never tell you to do right. For instance if you are going to a party the enemy will begin to rush you by telling you over and over again in your ear, "You are going to miss everybody and the party will be over when you get there, with your slow self!" In addition, the family members that are saved for real, you are going to stay out of their eyesight, not knowing you do not have to be in a person's face to see what is going on with an individual. God will show His sold out people.

Many people have not experienced a personal relationship in Christ and the enemy makes people think they are crazy. Baby, don't get it twisted. The problem is most pastors don't flow or operate in the spiritual realm but that doesn't mean they are not saved. Romans 10:9-10 states, that if you confess with your mouth the Lord Jesus died on the cross and believe in your heart that God has raised Him from the dead you will be saved.

Apostle Carolyn Edwards

Chapter 3

Turned Out

When you have tried everything and nothing is working in your favor, the enemy will pull your heart stings by placing thoughts in your mind of people you love and are close to. I never understood why people of God would go to their unsaved family and friends to ask a spiritual question. What trips me out is the Christian will wait on an answer as if it was revelation or knowledge coming straight from the throne of grace. These same deep church folks act like they never make a mistake or sin. People are being turned out on a daily basis, our mind goes straight to the prison but baby you got that thing twisted - you do not have to go to prison to get turned out, just attend church.

I would like to share a testimony with you about a man of God I met. He was married to a woman who wanted nothing out of life. The one thing that turned her on was raising hell with him on a daily basis, except she conceived a lot of children from their marriage. I promise you baby, we as a people can raise a $100 worth of sane toward each other, saying how much you hate each other but the next thing we hear is that she is pregnant with her sixth child. I heard of individuals saying "we may have argued a lot, but the makeup sex is a beautiful thing. When life's trials and tribulations hit a married couple's home, the romance suffers. You don't call me by my pet name any more. I can't do anything right for you, going to the park is out of the question, oh, and you said we can't hold hands in the park anymore because I'm an embarrassment to you. Well our most earnest problem is that we never have enough money to pay our bills. Now a demonic door is opened up and the various spirits enter into your mindset, such as depression, mental and physical sickness, then the pity party comes in the room. This happens because you stop praying and started finding fault with each other. The couple never realized it was only a smoke screen. The enemy likes to see God's people giving up on a promise. The devil will not have to worry about the people because God assigns an angel to protect those who are kingdom destination seekers.

Back to our testimony - The man of God's wife woke up one morning and informed her husband that she wanted a divorce, the love she used to have for him in her heart was gone. The man of God was broken. Now the next couple of years he went back to the streets trying to see if he still had some thunder down below, because he was angry and needed a release. The man remained committed to caring for his children - anybody can plant a seed, but a real man will never forget his responsibility (children).

One day the man of God woke up and decides he did not want to be broken anymore so he joined a mega ministry. After several weeks of attending his new church, his soul was filled with the word of God. Proverbs 3:8 says, "It shall be health to thy navel, and marrow to thy bones" - healing was taking place in his spirit. The man of God started rejoicing and joined the choir, usher board and the bible study group. The man of God felt complete within himself. Saints of God, when everything looks good in your life the enemy is lurking around the corner to set you up for a fall. On this Christian walk, you will find a lot of wolves in sheep clothing and believe it or not, most of the time the wolves are those in leadership of the church, the place God has designated for the healing of our soul to be restored, the enemy has turned church into corporate America. You never hear about believers getting filled with the Holy Ghost anymore, everybody is saved but no life style change.

Why do we keep looking for people to join the church? You act one way at home in front of your kids then at church you become a sanctified mess with much attitude trying to impress fake people, now your children are confused about the God you serve. You now have a new church building on every corner, but most of the churches are empty Back in the day you would see tent revivals on every corner, now you have TV ministry. I would like to ask a question: when you send the TV minister money, do they lay hands on you to deliver the condition in your body? Or if you need counsel for your issue will they take the time out to schedule an appointment for you? I never understood why some people join a big ministry but come to the small ministry for healing and deliverance. It is not good to use God's people, Psalms 105:15 says, "Touch not mine anointed, and do my prophets no harm." You might feel like I am snapping, but most homosexuals have multiple gifts. Some churches overlook the homosexual spirit because of the gifts God bless them with, the church should have sat them down and taught them the word of God. Please saints of God embrace the homosexual with love and affection; this will draw them close to the word of God. I promise if you make a change, a change will take place in their life.

The reason I know so much about the homosexual lifestyle is my husband and I first church was founded in Brooklyn, New York. The name of the church is Redemption Fellowship. The first service we had was on a Friday night, we had 27 people to join. 20 of them were homosexuals, 4 were prostitute and the last 3 were homeless. We labored with God's people, many believers asked me how could we teach homosexuals and I reply, "The same way you teach at any service, open your bible for the word of God." We had 4 Pastors to come out of that crowd.

Let's move on with this knowledge God is downloading in us - the enemy began to shift the man of God's focus to the men that were in the ministry. These men were bisexual with a position in leadership such as prophet, choir director, praise team leader, minister of music, and pastor. The devil was an archangel over the heavenly choir, one day he looked up to the third heaven were God resides and decided he wanted all power in his own hand, like God (The devil has convinced a whole world into thinking he does not exist). You know the story; Satan convinced 1/3 of God's angels to follow him so God kicked him and the angels out of heaven. Satan gets the glory out of trying to steal the show. For instance every time you see a choir director standing in front of his choir directing a song, why does he have to shake his butt so hard and poke his lips out? Watch your attitude, I hear what you are saying - "He could be happy in the spirit of God." True that, but why do some singers bend over touching their toes and shaking their behind while they are performing at a gospel service? It looks like a booty-call! Let me tell you something, when the anointing is on the scene for real, I don't care how it may be in a church service Satan and his imps will line up or they will get ghost. For the deep church folks that do not understand what "get ghost" means - they will leave.

21

Have you ever seen forbidden fruit that you knew was addictive and God warned you to stay away from it? The devil began to play that picture over and over in your mind like a re-run. Remember in the Garden of Eden, Genesis 3:2- 6, "and the woman said unto the serpent, we may eat of the fruit of the trees of the garden; but of the fruit of the trees which is in the midst of the garden, God hath said, Ye shall not eat of it, neither shall you touch it, lest ye die: and the serpent said to the woman, ye shall not surely die; for God doth know that in the day ye eat thereof, then your eye shall be opened, and ye shall be as gods, knowing good and evil. And when the woman saw the tree was good for food, and that it was pleasant to the eyes, and a tree to be desired to make one wise, she took of the fruit thereof, and did eat, and gave also unto to her husband with her; and he did eat." Back in the day of my grandparents, we were told to believe half of what you see and none of what we hear.

On one of those depressed days, he admitted to himself that he was still battling with the loss of his wife. The man of God went to church for a healing service that started at 7:30 pm, the word was awesome. Then one of the ministers had altar call. The man of God felt really good in his spirit so he decided that he would pray to seal everything in his heart that he had received from the Lord. He didn't want to lose any of the words God had spoken in his life. Check this mess out: the minister that prayed for the man of God was gay (the devil is a mess). Now he just receives an impartation of a homosexual spirit inside his very mind, body and soul. 1 Timothy 5:22, "Lay hands suddenly on no man, neither be partaker of other men, keep thyself pure." Children of God, we need to be careful who we allow to lay hands on us, I don't care if they are your kinfolks or friends. 1 John 4:1, "Beloved, believe not every spirit, but try the spirits whether they are of God: because many false prophets are gone out unto the world." A lot of saints have no discernment or insight, all that means is you cannot see in the spirit realm, so you depend on your flesh and carnal mind to answer a spiritual question.

Nowadays people go off of face value and that is why so many people keep getting church hurt. You put your trust in flesh and not in God. When we know better we should do better. 1 Thessalonians 5:12, "And we beseech you, brethren, to know them which labor among you, and are over you in the Lord, and admonish you." The man of God began to have dreams about having relations with the same sex; he was too embarrassed to tell anyone so he pays it no attention. Then he started feeling an attraction towards the same sex, he had no clue that the gay spirit had taken root in his very soul, he had developed an ungodly soul tie (An emotional, psychological, and physiological dependence an individual develops toward another person or thing. It is the captivation of one's mind and emotion and it is formed when one yields his body to a person or thing). Ungodly soul ties develop when we break God's law and engage in forbidden activities such as idolatry and sexual sin and it feeds on lust, idolatry, sorcery, and witchcraft. Proverbs 5:22, "His own iniquities shall take the wicked himself, and he shall be holden with the cords of his sins."

Well saints the man of God got set up by the "okie-doke" and fell with the gay pastor who had prayed for him in the first place. This affair went on for several months in that mega church. Don't get it twisted; this same abomination happens in the small churches too! This homosexual spirit is spreading like the invasion of the body shaker. Eventually, the pastor dropped the man of God like a hot potato, but he left him with a present for life – AIDS. After the fall, he began to have a lot of ungodly-sex with any man that wanted him sexually. The man of God was broken. I have a problem with this, how is it that the man can blame God for getting the AIDS virus. My father in heaven gets blamed for a lot of sinful things by his so-called people. Some Christians always justify their mess like that is not enough, but check this out these same people will try to back up their sin with scripture. The awesome God I serve "don't do" sin! And he doesn't hurt us, although he allows the enemy to test us. Always remember trials come to make us strong; new levels, new devils!

Wait a minute, a lot of women got turned out in these churches too. The saints in this day age have a lot of people's blood on their hands due to being abusive, rude, and putting their mouths on them. James 3:8, "But the tongue can no man tame; it is an unruly evil, full of deadly poison." Most people have experienced some kind of rape, molestation and rejection. I met a woman of God who grew up in an abusive home, her father was an alcoholic and her mother went to church. The woman of God experienced sex at a very early age, she was looking for a father in the wrong place. The enemy knew she had a major call on her life, so he used one of the closest things to her heart – her father. He began to abuse her mentally - She remembered the first time it happened and her whole world came tumbling down. She had lost respect for one of the most important people in her little life. Now life had no meaning and as she grew into her teenage years she began to abuse alcohol. I though this story couldn't get any worse, but then the woman of God got raped by a close family member; the enemy will keep knocking you down until you fight back.

Her testimony got worse before it got better; the young girl was at a bad point in her life. The enemy knew she had no more respect for herself and didn't care who she had ungodly sex with. The devil saw an opportunity to control her mind and took it by sending an older man in her life, she fell in "love" to the point, whatever that demon asked her to do she did it without giving it a second thought. Well you know he was not saved, he was a hot mess. That demon began to ask the young girl to perform (dance) in front of him with no clothes on and she did it, for the sake of love. After that he got his freak on, meaning, he had sex with her body in every position he could find. Then he laid a big burden on her little heart, he didn't want her to be his girlfriend anymore he needed to mess with her mind to see if he completely had her heart. She was devastated to the point of wanting to take her life. But when you have a calling on your life, God will always intervene by putting a sanctified person in your pathway to help you go to your next level, always remember it takes a Judas to push you into your next dimension! James 10:13, "There hath no temptation taken you but such as is common to man: but God is faithful, who will not suffer you to be tempted above that ye are able; but will with the temptation also make a way to escape, that ye may be able to bear it."

Well the girl got saved and started attending church with her mother, months went by she was happy in Jesus with her family. Weeks later on a beautiful day, her father got fired off his job took the little money he had in his pockets and got bent (I hate the devil) remember saints the devil don't have any new tricks he just uses different faces to knock us off our square.

Apostle Carolyn Edwards

Chapter 4

Down Low Brother or Sister

I would like to ask one question, what are you hiding from? If you like packing peanut butter or licking a stamp, that is your prerogative. If you are still in the closet your new name will be "Coward." The enemy's job is to put you into bondage by telling you over and over again this is not the way God created man or women to live. Some people will not be seen in public with you, family will disown you and so-called friends will talk about you. Many people were molested at a young age and the memories of the pain were too much to bear so they blocked out the embarrassment and shame of their past. Always remember your mind is the devil's playground - The butt-naked truth is some of those molested children are now grown and now abusing others through molestation. Molesters (people that want to have sex with young innocent children) need to feel in control of their own life, so they find a way to lure little children to them by giving them candy or playing like they are lost and our innocent children fall right in their hands. Our children don't know what danger is, most of the time our children are being hurt by someone in the family or a close friend of the family.

We have people that were molested still hunting the person that raped them. In our mind we say we would never do that to any one, only to wake up one day and realize you have become the very thing you hated all your little life a molester. Boo, check this out - the devil doesn't have any new tricks, he continues to use the same old tricks but different faces to bring you out of retirement. Why do you keep falling for the same old tricks, meaning you could have gotten your full deliverance. A demon knows a demon and a demon knows a true saint of God. Let me share something with you a demon spirit can't sit beside me comfortably in church. Because he knows I am the one "your mother warned you about!" I am a ghost buster in the spirit realm! If you had a demon fight, after your church service, who in your church would you take with you to the fight? The enemy knows most people are prideful and would rather go to hell than take a hand out from someone in church.

We used to share problems with our Pastor, because he was the one God appointed to watch over our soul. Have you ever been in a position where you shared something personal with your man of God and the very next Sunday it was preached across the pulpit? Honey, get over the hurt and live in God. People of God, please complete your assignment within that church. If you don't complete your assignment you will not be elevated in the spirit realm by God, so please go back to the church God put you in, I promise you when it is time to leave that same church you won't be ready to leave. Men will lift you up and when your gift starts to manifest those same men will find a way to set you down.

Today some bisexual people worship their Pastor more than they worship God. Most bisexual people like the feeling of both worlds (having sex with men and women) so they find a church where there is no condemnation or confliction coming out of the Pastor's mouth. The people know they are out of order but if the Pastor is serving ice cream and cake, that only delays you from your destination with God. A preacher once told me when I know better I should do better, it is up to you boo! You can go with the lie or walk in truth.

Oh I forgot we as a people hate truth. A true leader of God will minister deliverance to their people. Matthew 15:26, "But he answered and said, it is not meat to take the children's bread, and cast it to the dogs." The word of God is a double edged sword. After you have heard the word of God you should be wounded from God gutting every condition and bad spirit out of your body but that's only if you gave your total mind, body and soul over to your creator. When you go through deliverance bad spirits have to come out of your body. A lot of five-fold ministries don't do deliverance - When you go through the process of being cleaned, you will have mucus coming out of your nose, you will pass gas, your urine will come down, and thick liquid will come out of your mouth, when you are purging spirits out of your body. The people of God get fearful when deliverance is taking place so while many people have a gift that they were born with, most preachers can't teach about something they have never experienced. So, we had people walking around thinking they are crazy because they see things that aren't there and when they express their experiences to their leader the response is, "I'll get back with you later." Well, let's just say the subject was never bought up again. I hate to say it but a lot of men and women pastors are prostituting God's people and their gifts. Once they use you up they will drop you like a bad habit.

When I lived in Birmingham, Alabama, there were a lot of bisexual teachers in the high school. One of the young girls, I worked with as a school advocate, got caught in the girl's bathroom with her mouth on another females private part. I asked her why she went out like that, she responded by telling me they were the only people in that school who accepted her the way she was. She then said, "All I have to do is take care of their sexual needs. I am good at what I do and now all the cheerleaders, flag girls and majorettes know my name; I am finally popular." I reported this incident to the school principal. The school started an investigation on the different teachers. Come to find out, the gym teacher was taking a shower with the girls. Once she was caught by the school's security camera repeating the same trick my young client was turning in the bathroom. The gym teacher admitted she had been with the entire majorette squad, cheerleaders and the flag girls. Then she stated, "I was teaching the girls how to have fun without getting pregnant."

Apostle Carolyn Edwards

Chapter 5

After God Delivers Them, Will Their Appearance Change?

God has used me in deliverance over the years in so many people's lives. I have witnessed the process of so many men who came in the church switching but left out pimping, not for a man but for a woman. You have to be tired of being out the will of God. A tormenting spirit will begin to ride your back and you won't be able to sleep at night. You will then find yourself out of the house looking for something or somebody to turn a trick with and in your confused state of mind; you will allow a demon to "fix" your problem. What you don't realize is the enemy has set you up for a fall; you will end up in somebody's bed, car, backyard or jail, giving up your treats to a person or thing unaware of what kind of spirit they are housing and transferring into your body.

This homosexual spirit makes men and women appearance or features change into what they think they have become. The men bend their hand down, poke their lips out and twist their hips back and forth like a woman - they even change the tone of their voice. On the other hand the women pimp like a man, dress like a man and will buy a strap on (man private part) to satisfy their woman. The way I see this picture is, if you put a strap on, you might as will go get the real thing (man). But to God be the glory, all those prayers you sent up before God about your sons, husbands, friends and church brothers came to pass - even the time you thought you were wasting, praying for them has paid off and you can rest for a season.

The next thing that happened to these homosexuals was, they repented to God for living a backslidden lifestyle. They began to live a Holy life before God; the Lord began to give them little assignments to see if they would obey His voice. These homosexuals stayed in church eating, drinking and sleeping the word of GOD. Please don't get it twisted, these men were tried by satan on a daily basis - the enemy sent old lovers to them to try and bring the renewed men of God out of retirement. A few men went back into the homosexual lifestyle like a dog that goes back and eat his own vomit. The reason they went back is, God elevated these men in the church and called them into ministry. God can call you into ministry today but you might not use your gift until years later, you first have to be taught and trained in your gift. A lot of people get a little power from God and think they are ready for the world so, they leave the ministry thinking they are ready to preach, teach, and cast out demons only to find out they have no power. Then you will see them slowly coming back to visit "they say," next thing you know they are acting like they had never left the church - the devil is a liar; if they bit you once they will bite you again because they never went through true deliverance. Christians that won't admit the truth about themselves can never be trusted in the body of Christ and you will always find them in the middle of confusion. Also check this out, all that purging of spirits the homosexuals did for the last two years, have come back in them as soon as they went back into the homosexual lifestyle. Do we have any ghost-busters around in the body of Christ that will not charge a fee to help folks out of bondage for the fifth time? We cannot give up on an individual that keeps falling back into sin. You have to learn how to leave people at Gods feet's and stop carrying them around in your heart.

Once the homosexual is clean of all infirmities, males will walk with a pimp, their hands don't hang down like a female and their voice changes back to being low-pitched and there is no sign of a homosexual spirit in them. If you know someone that says they used to be in the life but God has delivered them from a homosexual spirit you should not be able to tell a spirit was ever in them. God does not make any mistakes; once He cleans you up and gives you a holy bath, there is no residue left in your body. Once they fall back into the unclean lifestyle all the signs will return back worse than before. Females, on the other hand, are a total different seed; they will grow their hair back, change their dress code back to being feminine and begin to hit on men as if they really want an honest relationship. Most men look at the outer appearance (figure) of a woman and get caught up in a relationship looking for fulfillment in the flesh. The butt-naked truth is, you will never fine fulfillment in sin. That is a make believe truth that the enemy has implanted in so many people's minds.

Here are some deliverance tools God will use to free His people from bondage:

a) Repent and ask God to forgive you of your involvement with any unclean evil spirit
b) Jesus' blood will cover you on a daily walk as long as you stay in the fold
c) Keep the word of God in your heart at all times, this will help you fight the enemy when the devil comes in your life like a flood
d) Forgiveness unlocks your next level

These are tools used by satan to put us in bondage:

a) People that ask you about your sex life
b) People that always talk about how good they are in bed

c) People that need to know about your marriage problems
d) Advice from a sinner about your rights as a wife

Apostle Carolyn Edwards

Chapter 6

Can They Counsel an Old Lover Without Falling Back Into Temptation?

When you come face to face with an old flame, the first thing the enemy wants to do is bring you out of retirement. If they are not saved for real, baby it's on! They are going to size you up to see if they can make anything jump or leap out of you. Baby, don't get that thing twisted, they know what turns you on so they are going to pull out all the old tricks just to see if they can still hook you. Please keep it real with yourself the enemy does not want you to be free. Misery loves company - if your life has been full of hurt, pain, disappointment, rejection, abandonment, all the mistakes you made over the years that still haunt you every time you close your eyes, and God only knows the scars and battle wounds you never heal from within now. Depression and suicidal thoughts hunt you constantly.

The next thing to look for is an all-out hit from every direction - lights got cut off in your home, car got repossessed, no food to feed the kids and all your money is gone. This test is designed for you to call it quits and give up on God. The enemy will send suicidal thoughts; you feel this might be your only way out. But God will not leave you in a time like this; trials come to make you strong! God knows how much we can bear. The only thing the enemy has on you is frustration, tiredness and your anxiety has kicked in triple time, you need to focus on first priorities, then on getting yourself together so you will be able to make stable decisions for you and your family. With everything that's going on in your life, you run into an old lover. Someone that used to rock your world, every Friday night when your children would go over to their grandparent's house for the weekend, while you were in school earning your degree. You must remember she knows every inch of your body, she knows how to turn you on and what gestures to use on you to get your attention. We always say "I will forgive you, but I will never forget" - my teacher informed me that when you remember the hurt/pain and you still have the same reaction in the body. You never forgave that individual.

Counseling an old lover - the truth of the matter is, if you have not been gutted out by God you will still have residue on you from the streets. It would be hard to counsel an old lover that you still have feelings for. I don't care if you say nothing is there, this homosexual demon is off the chain; it will size you up in one second. Then this spirit is so bold with its advances towards the same sex, if you are weak in any part of your body you'll fall for the okie-doke. This person allows all her problems to overwhelm her to the point of no return. The enemy has made her feel like all she needed was somebody to love on her body. I cannot imagine being in this position she feels like God would not have allowed her to run into this woman, after all these years have went by, unless God wanted this female to help the woman of God. Well you already know what took place! The woman that was sent to help her started out by giving her money for her bills, money for her children, extra spending change and of course it's been a long time since she had some free money to shop around with. After she spent all the money the old lover needed her to pay it back, but she did not want cash! The old lover asked the woman of God to submit her body to her for one hour and allow her to do anything she wanted with her body and everything would be over between the two of them. How many people have been at the mercy of an ungodly spirit?

The woman had to make a quick decision; you already knew he was talking in her ear. The problem was she thought the money came to her with no strings attached. She asked God what should she do, one voice said "Stand still and see the salvation of the Holy Ghost" and the other voice said "what is one hour? You need to be set free and you have not been with anyone for the last three years." The woman of God asked the old lover to give her time to fast to God before she commits to any kind of wrong act. Well people of God when the fast was over she slept with the old lover. I need to know, what God gave her permission to have sex with the same sex! I think she fasted to the wrong God! Saints please learn the word of God so no one can tell you any old thing about the dos and don'ts. The laws God gave us to live by each day of our lives are real.

A lot of people cannot tell their pastor is a homosexual because the people of God have no discernment. I had some people to tell me they would never go to a church were the pastor is a homosexual. If you don't know their story you can never share their glory. People in this day and age place judgment on each other. I never understood stuck up people who like hurting folk's feelings in the body of Christ; most of them have been abused and hurt. If we learn to look past flesh and see the spirit you will know what to pray for in each individual.

Chapter 7

If I Was Raped By the Same Sex, How Would I Get Rid of the Feeling, Desire and Ungodly Soul Tie?

D o not fool yourself into thinking that you got everything under control. The devil doesn't have any new tricks he just uses difference faces to get the job done. Here are some nuggets God downloaded for me to use so I could stay free:

- You have to go through a complete deliverance
- Living a life full of fasting and prayer
- Not entertaining/playing with spirits of your past
- You must keep the word of God in your belly on a daily basis
- You must have a communication line open with God at all times
- Surround yourself with people sold out for God
- Walk in truth
- Keep negative people out of your life
- You can't compromise anything small or great in God
- Be careful who you allow to lay hands on you

- Never be afraid to rebuke a demon that is trying to knock you off your square

Chapter 8
The Conclusion

During the many years of laboring in the body of Christ, God has used me to assist in true deliverance with so many shepherds and sheep. I have counseled many men and women who stated, they got caught up in a bad situation.

One pastor told me she got kicked out the house at age 15, with her baby, because a palm reader told her father his spells would never work as long as she was still in his house. The father believed what the palm reader said about his daughter and put her and her newborn baby out in the street. The young girl wandered in the streets, sleeping in cars, abandoned houses and wherever else she could find an empty spot in the streets to lay their heads. The young girl felt like a curse had been put on her and the baby. She remembered the God her mother prayed to before she died and she began to pray to God for favor.

One day she ran into an old friend of hers who invited her and the baby to her house for the night. You know the enemy is always looking to break somebody down, around 12 midnight the so-called friend went into the bedroom, where she allowed the young girl and her baby to sleep. The friend, who was a woman, woke the young girl up and told her she had to make love to her or she was going to put her and her baby out in the street. The young girl knew that she wasn't gay but it was her responsibility to take good care of her daughter so she made love to her supposed girlfriend.

When you are faced with a pastor who is undercover and refuses to get delivered, you have some praying to do. Our next series of books will provide additional tools in praying, exposing and staying under the will of God, while yet believing that God will convert and deliver his divine leader from the sin of homosexuality.